The Adventures of the Itty Bitty Frog

Kimberly P. Johnson

Illustrated by Scott Arnold

Pentland Press, Inc.
England • USA • Scotland

Foreword

Imagine a frog showing kindness to a lost bird. The author tells about the delightful adventures of an itty, bitty frog who helps a lost baby bird. Through ingenuity, courage and determination, the frog rescues the lost bird and safely returns him to his weeping mother. For the itty, bitty frog's good deed, Mother Bird praises him for honesty and kindness.

The illustrations are beautiful, and they help tell the story with deep feelings!

Ruby Swinson Murchison, Ed.D.
Veteran Educator
Former National Teacher of the Year

Kim Johnson has used her knowledge of children to write an entertaining story about courage and the importance of keeping a promise in a manner that all children can understand. This delightfully written and illustrated book has great potential as an educational tool for young children. I hope that this is only the first of many books authored by Kim.

Dr. Deborah Whaley
Department Chairperson
Early Childhood Education
Fayetteville Technical Community College

This book is dedicated to Mom, Dad and Travis for always believing in me;

to Jeff for his constant love and support;

and most of all, God, for making everything happen!

-KPJ

To my parents, Dick and Donna Arnold, your unconditional love and support have been my motivation in life.

To Debbie and Becky and Grammy May; To Jim, thank you, thank you!

And to Dan Ofsthun, our friendship was so dear to me, I will never forget you.

77*823*143

-SDA

PUBLISHED BY PENTLAND PRESS, INC.
5124 Bur Oak Circle, Raleigh, North Carolina 27612
United States of America
919-782-0281

ISBN 1-57197-062-2
Library of Congress Catalog Card Number 97-65963

Copyright © 1997 Kimberly P. Johnson
Illustrated by Scott Arnold

Printed in Hong Kong

Down by the river, in the coolness of the light,
was an itty, bitty frog that had been there all night.

He skimpered and he scampered through the grass so green.
He was the cutest little frog you had ever seen!

He hopped
and he hopped
through the fields
so tall,

and he chatted with the mice
as they sat on the wall.

3

The frog waved at the bees as they buzzed along,

and he listened to
the crickets as they played their song.

4

Then the itty, bitty frog had just stopped for a rest,
when he saw a little bird that had fallen from his nest!

The bird lay crying at the bottom of the tree.
He shouted out loudly, "Please help me!"

6

Well, the frog hopped over to the tiny, little bird.
"Are you the one shouting? Are you the one I heard?"

The bird nodded his head
and stuck out his chest,
"Yes, I'm the one you heard.
I fell from my nest!

When I fell from my nest, I began to roam.
Now it looks as if I'm a long way from home."

Then the frog looked down and said
with a sigh,
"Hush little bird, there's no need to cry.

I'll get you home to the top of the tree.
Don't worry about a thing. Just leave it to me!"

The baby bird said, "Thanks. I don't mean to complain,
but I'm awfully scared and it looks like rain!"

So the frog made a bed to keep the bird dry.
He turned his head up and looked towards the sky.

It was a long way up to the top of the nest,
but the frog was determined to give it his best!

He hopped and he hopped until his legs grew sore,
and he searched and he searched
until he couldn't anymore.

The itty, bitty frog sat down to think for a while when he heard a faint cry—"Where is my child?"

The frog ran into the woods to see who it could be.
It was the sad mama bird sitting high in a tree.

She had tears in her eyes
and a broken heart, too.
She had looked all over and didn't know what to do.

The frog jumped up and yelled loudly,
"Look down here, mama bird, at the bottom of the tree.
I found your baby and he's not too far from here.
He's lying safely tucked away, so there's no need to fear."

"I'll go and get him as quickly as I can."
The frog turned to hop away and then the rain began.

At first, it started slowly with just a drop or two,
and then the sky grew tired of that and let the rain pour through.

But this didn't stop
the itty, bitty frog as he hopped along the trail.
He had to get the birdy home. He didn't want to fail.

The bird chirped loudly
  with excitement and with glee,
    "Thank you, Mr. Frog. You're so kind to help me!"

The frog took the baby to the smiling mama bird.
She said, "You are an honest frog
because you really kept your word."

The frog smiled back and said, "I didn't mind.
I wish everyone we met could be a little kind."

Then the itty, bitty frog turned around
in the coolness of the light,
to happily tuck himself away
for a very pleasant night.

The End